W9-AVK-590

BIBLES
AND
BESTIARIES

BIBLES AND BESTIARIES

A Guide
to Illuminated Manuscripts

Elizabeth B. Wilson

The Pierpont Morgan Library

Farrar, Straus and Giroux

New York

To my parents

Frontispiece:
"Marriage of the Virgin," from a Book of Hours by the Master of Morgan 453, M.453, f.30v.

Published simultaneously in Canada by HarperCollins*CanadaLtd*
Printed and bound in Italy by Arnoldo Mondadori Editore
First edition, 1994
Photography: David A. Loggie, The Pierpont Morgan Library
This publication was supported in part by grants from the National Endowment
for the Arts, a federal agency, and the Joseph H. and Florence A. Roblee
Foundation.

Library of Congress Cataloging-in-Publication Data

Wilson, Elizabeth B.
   Bibles and bestiaries : a guide to illuminated manuscripts /
Elizabeth B. Wilson. — 1st. ed.
     p. cm.
   At head of title: The Pierpont Morgan Library.
   Includes bibliographical references.
   1. Illumination of books and manuscripts, Medieval — Juvenile literature.   2. Bible. N.T.—
Illustrations—Juvenile literature.   3. Bestiaries in art—Juvenile literature.   4. Illumination of books
and manuscripts—New York (N.Y.)—Juvenile literature.   5. Pierpont Morgan Library—Juvenile
literature. [1. Illumination of books and manuscripts.]   I. Pierpont Morgan Library.   II. Title.
ND2920.W56 1994
745.6'7'0902—dc20
          94-6687
          CIP
          AC

Table of Contents

Monks at Work on an Illuminated Manuscript

1. Shown above are the royal owners of this manuscript, the great crusader-king Louis IX of France and his mother, Blanche of Castile.

Introduction

Nowadays books are everywhere and within reach of even the most modest incomes. Books are mass-produced on sophisticated printing machinery that can duplicate texts and images in a matter of seconds. It is not unusual for a million copies of a single book to be printed at one time, and books exist on every conceivable subject, from aardvarks to zippers.

During the Middle Ages, however, the way books were made and the role they played in culture was quite different. There were no printing presses and all books had to be written out by hand. We call such books MANUSCRIPTS, from the Latin *manus*, meaning hand, and *scribere*, to write. Any illustrations or decorations were also drawn or painted by hand. These manuscript paintings were often embellished with real gold or silver and are called ILLUMINATIONS (from the Latin word *lumen*, light) because the shiny metals caught and reflected light (fig. 1). Books were not merely a source of information. They often were meant to be works of art in their own right.

The production of an ILLUMINATED MANUSCRIPT could take several years to complete. (Think of how long it would take you to write out the Bible.) The cost of a very large and lavishly illustrated book could be about the same as for the construction of a medium-sized cathedral. Understandably, a book was one of the most precious objects a person could own. A German manuscript Bible contains the following warning, which may amuse us today but was meant in all seriousness: "If anyone take away this book, let him die the death; let him be fried in a pan; let the falling sickness and fever seize him; let him be broken on the wheel and hanged. Amen."

Throughout most of the Middle Ages, the owners of books were an elite minority—primarily members of the Church and the nobility. Not only was the cost of books prohibitive for almost anyone else, but very few people could read or write in the first place. It is estimated that during the tenth century only about five percent of the population of Europe was literate. (The great emperor Charlemagne was quite proud of his ability to read but never was able to master writing.)

Nevertheless, a very large number of books were produced during the Middle Ages. In fact, more books survive from the medieval period than any other single type of object. Preserved today in museums, libraries, churches, and private collections around the world, illuminated manuscripts are our best link with this long and fascinating period. They give us a ringside seat at battles and banquets, stag hunts and church services, weddings and funerals. They tell us what people prayed for and feared, how they worked and what they did for fun, what kind of clothes they wore, what weapons they used, what they ate and drank—in short, they tell us what life was really like in the Middle Ages (figs. 2–4).

Medieval Warfare

2. Medieval artists often depicted events from the Bible as if they were taking place in their own time. In this thirteenth-century manuscript, the armies of the Hebrew king Saul are dressed like French knights on crusade in the Holy Land. The soldiers wear shirts and leggings of mail, and metal helmets with slits for viewing. In the margin of the page, a man clings to a *trebuchet*, a kind of catapult used by attacking armies to breach walls.

The text at the bottom of the page is in Latin, but if you look carefully at the margin of the page, you can also see Persian writing. Several centuries after this book was made, it was owned by Shah Abbas of Persia, who had his scribes write captions for the paintings.

3. Knights and ladies prepare to dine on peacock, in a scene from this fourteenth-century French manuscript of a courtly poem.

4. A fourteenth-century German manuscript depicts the construction of the Tower of Babel, but shows workers using medieval techniques.

5. Vikings in their "dragon ships" invading Britain by sea, from a twelfth-century English manuscript.

In the Beginning . . .

The term *Middle Ages* suggests an in-between time, and it was. The Middle Ages was a period of about one thousand years, between the collapse of the Roman Empire during the fifth century A.D. and the revival of classical art and learning known as the Renaissance around the fifteenth.

The ancient Romans created one of the most sophisticated and highly organized civilizations the world has ever known. At its height, their empire extended throughout most of Europe and into parts of Africa and Asia. But by the late fourth century, the Roman Empire had begun to weaken and disintegrate. Successive waves of barbarian invasions hastened its end. Among the most feared tribes were the Goths, the Huns, and the Vandals, whose reputation for senseless destruction survives in our English word *vandalism*. In time, much of Europe looked like a ghost town. Living in huts among the crumbling ruins of Roman temples and aqueducts, people eked out the most primitive type of existence. Fear of attack by barbarians was a part of life (fig. 5).

During this dark and chaotic period, small groups of devout Christians came together and sought out remote, inaccessible places where they could live with a measure of security and pursue a religious life. Some of the earliest of these monastic communities were established along the bleak and rocky coast of western Ireland and in the deserts of Egypt, in northern Africa.

These people were doing something that almost no one else could do at the time—reading and writing. And they were making something that almost no one else could make or had any use for—books. Christianity, like Judaism and Islam, is a religion of the written word. The Bible is regarded as a sacred text, containing the revealed truth of God. The most important part of early monastic life was the preservation, reading, and copying of these texts. From the beginning, books and monks were inseparable.

And also from the very beginning, we find them devoting much time to the decoration of the pages and bindings of these sacred texts (figs. 6–8). The early Christian monks and nuns lived a life of great austerity and simplicity. No personal possessions were allowed, and they wore simple robes made of coarse cloth. Yet

An Early Christian Manuscript from Egypt

6. This is one of the earliest surviving examples of an illustrated Christian manuscript. It was made in Egypt during the fifth century. The artist has combined the Christian cross with the Egyptian life symbol, the ankh (☥).

Binding for a Manuscript

7. Goatskin binding for a gospel book dating from the seventh or eighth century. It was found buried in the ruins of an ancient monastery in the Fayum region of Egypt. The cover is decorated with tooled designs and different-colored leathers.

they felt that the word of God should be adorned, embellished, and reproduced using the finest possible materials.

Although Christianity rejected the pagan religion of the ancient Romans, early Christian art, culture—and books—owed much to them. Latin, the Roman language, became the official language of the Church and of the books that the Church produced. This had a real practical advantage, for it meant that monks from different countries could communicate with one another and read the same books (fig. 9).

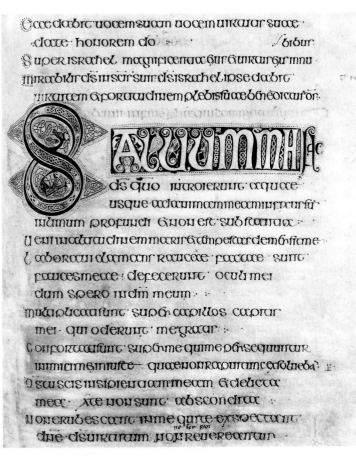

Decorated Letters from an English Manuscript

8. A page from an eighth-century English manuscript of the Psalms. The Latin word *salvum* (save) is enlarged and decorated to mark the beginning of a new section. Inside the *S* is a dragon, and various bird-like and human forms are contained in the rest of the letters. The style of such manuscripts was influenced by the decorative animal forms found in Viking art.

Pessime mus!

9. The monk Hildebertus spies a pesky mouse (*mus*) stealing his piece of cheese. He notes his anger—in Latin—in the manuscript on his desk. "*Pessime mus, sepius me provocas ad iram, ut te deus perdat!*" (Cursed mouse, you anger me so often—God take you!) At his feet his young apprentice, Everwinus, practices painting the kinds of foliage designs used in the borders of manuscripts.

13

11. The first-century Roman emperor Caesar Augustus issues a decree, from a fifteenth-century Italian manuscript.

From Scroll to Codex

10. Instead of using scrolls for their writings, early Christian monks adopted the codex form, with individual leaves stitched together. In this ninth-century manuscript, the gospel writer St. Luke holds a codex, while at his feet is a basket with scrolls.

The early Christians also adopted a new type of book that the Romans had developed. It was quite different from the traditional scrolls that were commonly used throughout the ancient world. It was square-shaped and consisted of individual folded pages that were sewn together and could be turned one at a time. This form of book is called a CODEX (fig. 10). It probably evolved from the ancient practice of sometimes writing on wooden tablets filled with wax. (The word *codex* comes from the Latin *caudex*, meaning a block of wood.) We know that by the first century A.D., Romans began to use the codex for certain kinds of writing, although much of their literature was still produced in the form of scrolls (fig. 11).

Why did the Christians so specifically choose the codex for their books? No one is entirely sure. The most obvious answer is that it was more practical for their purposes than the scroll. Imagine trying to use the telephone book in scroll form. The codex could be handled easily and specific passages could be located more quickly for reading and study. When finished, the codex was simply shut. The scroll had to be rerolled. The codex was also more compact and economical, since both sides of the writing surface could be used, while scrolls were left blank on one side.

Although the early Christians did not invent the codex, we can thank them for making it the standard book form used throughout the world today.

Christianity slowly spread from these tiny outposts in Egypt and Ireland to become one of the most powerful and pervasive forces in Europe. And wherever the Christian monks and missionaries went, they brought books and the art of bookmaking with them. Just as their churches grew ever more elaborate and richly decorated, so, too, their books became ever more lavishly painted with colors and gold (fig. 12).

A Priest and Two Deacons Celebrate Mass

12. This book contains the texts and anthems to be read and sung by the priest during the service. It was made during the fourteenth century.

13. During the later Middle Ages, illuminated manuscripts were commonly produced for the instruction and pleasure of the nobility. This fifteenth-century manuscript is written in French and includes various myths and legends from ancient history. Here the Greek beauty Helen greets King Priam of Troy.

For many centuries, the Church remained the center of all learning and literacy in Europe, and the vast majority of books were made by and for the Church. In time, however, the art of reading, writing, and bookmaking passed outside the monastery and into the court and town. Books came to reflect nearly every aspect of medieval life. Books also began to be written in the VERNACULAR, that is, the spoken language of a particular country, such as English, German, or French. Books changed as the medieval world changed, but the tradition of making them as beautiful as possible in every way continued well into the Renaissance and into the age of the printing press (fig. 13).

Byzantine Manuscript

14. St. Mark, from a manuscript made in Constantinople in the eleventh century. It is written in Greek, the official language of the Byzantine Empire.

OTHER "PEOPLE OF THE BOOK"

While much of Western Europe was struggling to bring some sense of order and continuity to people's lives, a brilliant and highly cultured civilization flourished in the lands of the Byzantine Empire to the east. Its capital, Constantinople, had been established on the site of the ancient Greek city of Byzantium. Constantine, the first Roman emperor to convert to Christianity, renamed the city for himself, and it became the second, eastern capital of the Roman Empire. It was also an important center for the Christian religion and the making of books. (The Christian Church of the Byzantine Empire survives today in the Greek Orthodox religion.)

The Byzantines were famed for the beauty and lavishness of their palaces and churches. The ceiling of their great church of Hagia Sophia was overlaid with pure gold; sunlight flooding the huge dome lit up the richly colored marble floors and walls of the interior. This love of splendor and richness is reflected in their manuscripts (fig. 14).

Although Christianity dominated much of Europe during the Middle Ages, there were also large communities of Jewish people in nearly every European country. Like the Christians, Jews were also "people of the book" and had a great respect for literacy and learning. The Hebrew Bible, which includes the TORAH (the first five books of the Old Testament) and other writings, was central to the spiritual life of every Jew. Reading from the Torah was and is a standard part of their faith.

We have seen how the early Christians adopted the codex form and made it the standard type of book by the fifth century. However, medieval Jews continued to use the scroll for another five hundred years or more. Why? No one really knows. The Jewish religion is much older than that of the Christians. Perhaps Jews considered it a matter of pride and reverence for their ancient, sacred writings to continue to copy them in the traditional scroll form. (The Torah is still produced today in the scroll form for use in synagogues.) By the end of the tenth century, however, Jews had begun to make books in codex form. And in time they, too, adorned their manuscripts with elaborate painted decorations and gold (fig. 15).

A Hebrew Bible

15. The opening of the Book of Genesis, from a Hebrew Bible made in France during the fifteenth century. The Hebrew for "In the beginning" has been written entirely in gold.

Illuminated Koran

16. This delicately illuminated page is from the Koran, the sacred book of Islam, and dates from the mid-fourteenth or early fifteenth century.

During the seventh century, a new religion appeared in the East, which spread rapidly and soon came to dominate a vast area from Spain to India. This was the Islamic faith, which is based on the teachings of the prophet Mohammed. The followers of Mohammed are called Muslims and their holy book is the KORAN (fig. 16). According to Mohammed, the words of the Koran are the actual words of God speaking. These words are treated as sacred objects and Muslims believe that by copying the Koran they will earn heavenly reward.

Although it was common practice to include illustrations in the text of Christian Bibles, the Islamic faith does not permit representations of human beings or animals in the Koran. Instead, the makers of these books excelled in the perfection of a beautiful script and in creating intricate and elegant decorative patterns. On the other hand, the nonreligious books produced in Islamic countries are full of delightful scenes of the world around them. See, for example, the illustrations from a Persian bestiary on pages 35 and 44.

17. A French hunting manual

The Making of an Illuminated Manuscript

Seeing an illuminated manuscript for the first time can be a startling experience. Even though the book may be many centuries old, it often looks as if it had been produced only yesterday (fig. 17). The colors are vivid and pure. The gold is brilliant and shining. The pages are smooth and white. And the lettering is crisp and clear.

The remarkable state of preservation in which we find these manuscripts is largely due to the fact that they have spent most of their long lives closed up and protected from the damaging effects of light and the atmosphere. They were regarded as precious objects by their early owners and often kept in a treasury. (Nowadays, illuminated manuscripts are exhibited only for a few months at a time and under low artificial light.)

However, the fine condition of so many illuminated manuscripts is also a result of the extraordinary craftsmanship and care that went into every step of book production.

The creation of an illuminated manuscript was carried out in a series of very distinct stages and required the coordinated efforts of several skilled artisans: the vellum maker, the scribe, the illuminator, and the binder. During the course of the Middle Ages, there were great changes in the styles of writing and decoration, in the kinds of persons who made and used books, and in the types of manuscripts that were read. Yet the basic way a book was created remained virtually the same for more than a thousand years.

THE ART OF THE VELLUM MAKER

The first stage in the production of a manuscript was the preparation of the pages. These were not made of paper but of specially prepared animal skin called VELLUM or PARCHMENT. Usually the skins of sheep, goats, or calves were used (fig. 18).

The terms *vellum* and *parchment* are now used interchangeably. The word *parchment* comes from the ancient Greek city of Pergamum, whose king, Eumenes II, is said to have invented it during the second century B.C. The word *vellum* comes from the Latin word for calf, *vitellus*.

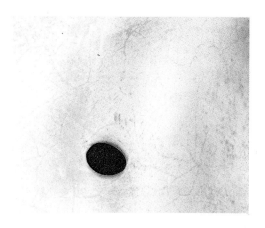

Vellum Skin

18. Vellum is still made today and used for certain kinds of important documents. (People used to refer to getting their college or high school diplomas as "getting that sheepskin.") This piece of modern vellum comes from a goat. The hole in the skin was probably made by a tiny cut during the scraping process.

Sources of Vellum: Sheep, Goats, and Calves

19. It is very unlikely that animals were ever slaughtered solely for the purpose of making vellum. Skins were a standard by-product of monastic and village kitchens.

We can imagine that the abbey butcher was a good source of supply for fresh skins in the monastic production of parchment. By the thirteenth century, commercial parchment makers were found in most towns and villages of any size (fig. 19). The number of skins needed for a manuscript book, of course, depended on the size of the book and the size of the animal. A very large Bible might require over two hundred full-grown sheep.

Preparing vellum was an enormously time-consuming, labor-intensive—and smelly—process. First, the skins were rinsed in running water for a day or so to clean them. They were then soaked in a solution of water and lime—a caustic chemical—for several days to loosen the hair. The parchment maker then scraped away the hair with a knife, being careful not to make any nicks or tiny gashes. The skins were rinsed and stretched on wood frames to dry. While on the stretchers, the skins were scraped yet again and rubbed several times to make them thin and even (fig. 20).

The goal was a smooth and uniformly white surface, but close examination of nearly every vellum page reveals some imperfections. Insect bites and old scars caused discolorations. In addition, as the skins were drying on stretchers, they would shrink. At this stage, cuts or weaknesses in the skin could turn into large holes. On some manuscript pages we can see quite clearly where these holes have been mended by stitching (figs. 21–22). Very often, though, the holes were simply left and written around.

Parchment Maker at Work

20. A modern parchment maker stretches a wet skin across the wood frame for drying. As skin sizes vary, the pegs are adjustable, like tuning pegs on a guitar.

King and Queen Playing Chess

21. The two stitched repairs in the lower section of this manuscript page are clearly visible.

Purple Vellum

23. The pages from this tenth-century manuscript have been painted purple and the text is written entirely in gold. Note the tiny hole in the vellum at the top, between the two columns of text.

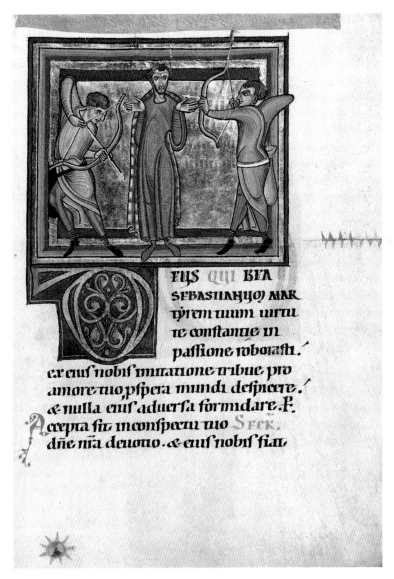

Embroidered Repairs to a Vellum Page

22. In this German manuscript, the holes and slits in the vellum have been stitched with a beautiful embroidery pattern of colored threads.

For the most sumptuous manuscripts, the vellum might be painted or dyed purple, the royal color. The purple page made a dazzling background for gold lettering and also conveniently masked most blemishes on the skin (fig. 23).

Once prepared, the vellum would be folded and cut to make the pages for the manuscript. Depending on the size of the pages needed, a single skin might be folded in half, quarters, or even smaller.

Ruling the Page

24. The ruled lines for the text and margins of a page were usually drawn with ink or marked with a sharp object, which would leave a crease on one side and a ridge on the other. But in this manuscript some of the rulings were done in gold! The pinpricks used as guides for the ruling are clearly visible in the margin of the page.

Before the actual writing could begin, the page had to be ruled to make margins and guidelines for the lines of the text. Ruling each page individually was tedious, and various ways were found to shorten the process. A common one was to take a stack of vellum leaves, measure out the top one, and then prick holes for the ruling pattern all the way through the stack of leaves. These small pinholes are still visible on many manuscript pages (fig. 24).

A Medieval Scriptorium

25. The scriptorium in the tower of the monastery of Tavara, Spain, is pictured in this thirteenth-century manuscript. One scribe sits at his work. Another uses a compass to rule a page. To the right, a young apprentice is trimming vellum with scissors.

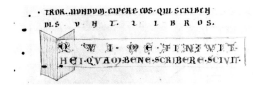

The Words of the Scribe

26. The scribe's note in this thirteenth-century Austrian manuscript is written in Latin and translates: "He who finished me, hey, how well he could write" (*Qui me finivit / Hei quam bene scribere scivit*).

THE ART OF THE SCRIBE

Once the vellum leaves were prepared and ruled, the next step was the writing of the text. The person whose job it was to copy the text was called a *SCRIBE* and the special room set aside for the writing of manuscripts was called a *SCRIPTORIUM* (fig. 25). In monasteries these were usually rooms with large windows for plenty of light, and good heating, since cold, cramped fingers simply don't write very well. Silence was strictly maintained. Communication was by signal, so as not to distract other scribes at work. When a monk needed another book to work on, he held out his hands, as if turning pages.

Scribes trained for many years to develop graceful and uniform handwriting, and they were respected members of the monastic community. St. Patrick, the great early Christian missionary in Ireland, took great pride in his abilities as a scribe. Another early Irish missionary, St. Columba, was even more famous. Legend has it that he once stayed up all night in a church copying a manuscript, and as he wrote his fingers glowed like candles, filling the church with a brilliant light.

When the task was complete, the scribe might sign his or her name at the end of the manuscript. (Thanks to these signatures, we have learned that a number of scribes were women.) Sometimes the scribes added a humble prayer of thanks to God or wrote of their pride in their work (fig. 26). On the other hand, quite a number expressed relief at being finished, complaining that their backs hurt and that the book was far too long!

We should not, by the way, think of scribes as writers in the modern sense of those who compose works of literature. Generally speaking, the job of a scribe was to copy exactly the text of an existing manuscript (fig. 27). The only way you could get a book was to have someone copy it for you or to write it out yourself.

Pens were made from the feathers, or quills, of large birds, usually geese or

27. A scribe copies out the text of a book that is propped up on a lectern above.

28. St. Mark is shown sharpening his pen with a knife in this fifteenth-century French manuscript.

Clever Corrections

29. A phrase was accidentally left out of the text in this manuscript. In the margin, a man and a funny creature move the words into position, while another fellow helpfully points to the spot where they should go.

30. Four whole lines were omitted from this page. Three men have tied a rope to the missing section and are hoisting it up into place.

St. John with His Portable Inkwell

31. St. John squints to check the sharpness of his pen as he writes the Book of Revelation. Illustrated here is the popular medieval legend that a devil tried to steal or knock over the saint's portable inkwell to keep him from writing the last book of the Bible.

swans. (Our word *pen* comes from the Latin word for feather, *penna*.) Quill cutting to form the right kind of pen point, or nib, was an art in itself. A sharp knife was used to pare away each side of the tip, with a final horizontal cut across the top. This area got the most wear, and a busy scribe would have to sharpen his quill many times during the course of a day's work (fig. 28). This is why medieval pictures of scribes nearly always show them with both a quill and a knife at hand.

The knife was also used to scrape away mistakes. If mistakes weren't caught in time to be scraped away, corrections were made in the text or in the margin of the page. Sometimes these corrections were made in a humorous or witty way (figs. 29–30). It's nice to know that these scribes could laugh at their mistakes.

The principal ink colors used were black and red. Black ink was used primarily for the text; red was usually used to show chapter headings and other divisions in the text. Medieval inks were much thicker and richer in color than our modern inks. Black carbon ink was made from charcoal or the soot from a candle. The carbon would be mixed with gum arabic, a substance made from the dried sap of the acacia tree.

Another kind of black ink was made from oak galls. Also called oak apples, these are small round growths formed when a gall wasp lays eggs in the growing bud of an oak tree. Oak galls are still found quite commonly on leaves and twigs of shrub oaks. Red ink could be made from vermilion (a combination of mercury and sulfur) or from chips of the brazilwood tree.

Preparatory Drawings for Manuscript Paintings

32. Several figures in the border of this manuscript page never got beyond the underdrawing stage, including these sketches for a music-making angel and a man and a bear.

Quill pens cannot hold a great deal of ink, so a good supply was always kept close at hand. Pictures of scribes in manuscripts usually show some kind of ink pot nearby or being held in the hand (fig. 31). Hollowed-out bull horns, which could be inserted into holes in the scribe's desk, were commonly used to hold ink.

THE ART OF THE ILLUMINATOR

As explained earlier, the painted decorations for a manuscript are called illuminations, and the artists who paint them are called illuminators. The term derives from the frequent use of gold or silver, which reflected light and literally made the page appear to be lit from within. Not all manuscripts were decorated with gold, but the term has now come to mean any kind of painted decoration in a manuscript.

The illuminations were carefully planned out ahead of time and sketches were made to serves as guides. Occasionally, the decorations of a manuscript were left unfinished, permitting us a rare glimpse of some of these artists' underdrawings (fig. 32).

In addition to framed paintings, the borders of manuscript pages and the initial letters of the texts were decorated. In fact, these are often the most delightful parts of a manuscript page. Borders might be painted to resemble lacelike patterns of vines and flowers in which tiny animals and figures lurk (fig. 33). Or they might contain little images which clarified the text (fig. 34).

A Decorated Border

33. Detail of a border showing a rabbit doctor and his patients, two dogs on crutches. (This may be the first rabbit in the history of art that wears glasses.)

34. This lively scene of peasants baking decorates a page of prayers to St. Philip, the patron saint of pastry makers.

36. To make an even right-hand margin, the illuminator has filled in the lines with a menagerie, including a rabbit and a dog, as well as a bishop with a giant foot.

A Historiated Initial

35. This page from an Italian choir book is a beautiful example of a historiated initial. The scene of the Nativity is framed by a giant letter *P*, which begins the sentence *Puer Natus Est Nobis* (Latin for *A child is born to us*). At the bottom of the stem of the *P*, an angel tells shepherds tending their flocks of the birth of Jesus. Curled up amid the leaves in the bottom right of the page, a lone shepherd plays his bagpipe.

Initial letters of words were also often given elaborate and intricate designs. A common type of letter decoration was the *HISTORIATED INITIAL*. This is a letter that was made very large and used to frame a scene or "history" (fig. 35). Another place where decorations occur is at the ends of lines of text. When a line didn't reach all the way to the margin, this space might be filled in with ornaments or bizarre and amusing tiny creatures (fig. 36).

It can be quite fun for us—as it undoubtedly was for the original owners of these manuscripts—to spend a long time studying the illuminations and finding all the hidden figures. But we should not forget that manuscript illumination had a very practical function as well. The decoration of letters helped readers find their way through the text by announcing the beginning of a new section or paragraph. The painted scenes would help explain the text, and this is important when we realize that many owners of manuscripts were barely literate themselves.

Making Gold Leaf

37. A gold-beater hammers out gold leaf from coins.

Gold was an important and expensive feature of manuscript illumination. Sometimes the gold was ground to a powder and used like paint. A more brilliant result was achieved by using gold leaf, which is gold that has been beaten into tissue-thin leaves. How thin? One source tells us that 145 leaves, each probably about a few inches square, could be beaten from a single gold coin (fig. 37). The gold leaf would be glued to the surface of the vellum page and then polished to a bright shine by a process called burnishing. Usually a smooth, hard object, such as an animal tooth, was used for burnishing. Gold leaf was always applied before other painting so that the burnishing process would not smudge or damage the surrounding painted areas (fig. 38). Unlike silver, gold will not tarnish,

An Unfinished Manuscript

38. These unfinished pages show the different stages in the creation of an illuminated manuscript. The pages have been ruled and the text has been written; gold leaf for the initial letters and border decoration has been applied and burnished; the painting of the border has begun, one color at a time.

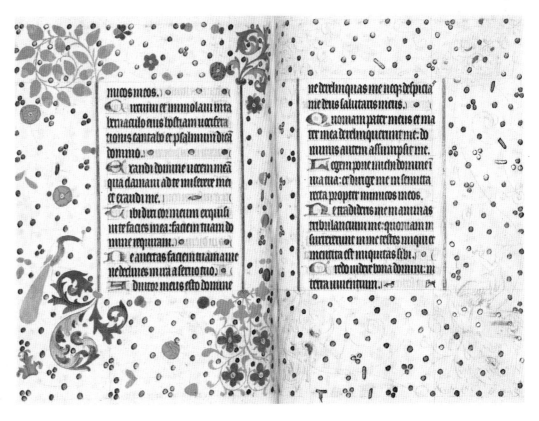

Burnished Gold Leaf

39. Here St. Martin is dividing his cloak with a beggar, from a thirteenth-century German manuscript. Although gold will not tarnish, it can become scratched. The little silk curtain sewn onto the vellum above the illumination protected the gold leaf and the delicate paints.

and the gold leaf in manuscripts sparkles as if it were new (fig. 39).

Illuminators vied with one another to create the most beautiful colors possible (fig. 40). Recipes for special colors were closely guarded secrets. A highly prized brilliant blue was made from crushing lapis lazuli, a semiprecious stone that came from Afghanistan and was more expensive than gold. A wide variety of reds were made from different kinds of plants and minerals. One very deep rich red was called dragon's blood, because in ancient times people thought it came from the blood of dragons. It was actually derived from a special kind of shrub grown in India. A beautiful yellow could be made from the stigmas of crocus blossoms. To make the paint the ground pigments were combined with glair, a liquid made from egg whites. Gum arabic was also a popular binder for colors.

The grinding of colors and the making of the paints was a tedious and time-consuming process. It was no doubt often turned over to novice monks and young apprentices.

40. The colors in this fifteenth-century French manuscript are exceptionally rich and finely made. The central miniature depicts the marriage of the Virgin. The surrounding medallions represent scenes from her birth and childhood.

41. The boards of this volume were never covered with leather. The manuscript leaves are sewn onto leather thongs, which are threaded into holes in the boards.

THE ART OF THE BINDER

When the text and decorations were finally complete, the manuscript was ready for binding. The folded pages were stacked up and sewn together with thick thread. (Some books—like the one that you are reading right now—are still bound that way today.) The sewn manuscript would then be fitted with sturdy covers, usually made of wooden boards, that were often covered and decorated in some way (fig. 41).

Leather covering was often used and could be stamped or tooled in a pattern (fig. 42). Cloth, such as velvet or silk, might be used as well, with an embroidered design.

For very important books, such as manuscripts for emperors or bishops, metal covers of gold or silver inlaid with jewels might be made. These "treasure bindings" are often as valuable as the manuscript itself (fig. 43).

Tooled Leather Binding

42. This binding covers a fifteenth-century Hebrew Bible. The large metal ornaments (also called bosses) at the corners and in the center protect the tooled leather when the book is opened.

A Treasure Binding

43. Gilt silver and jeweled book cover on a thirteenth-century German manuscript. In the center is a small statuette of the Virgin and Child. In each of the four corners, a gospel writer is shown at work. St. Mark, in the lower left, can be identified by his symbol, the lion. The little fellow standing next to St. Mark is Abbot Berthold of Weingarten Abbey, who commissioned this magnificent book and proudly had himself included on the cover.

Manuscript Painting of the Early Middle Ages

44. (*above left*) St. Luke, from a twelfth-century English gospel book. The saint is seated on his symbol, the ox, but both he and his writing stand seem to hover in midair.

An Italian Renaissance Manuscript

45. (*above right*) St. Luke, from a fifteenth-century Italian prayer book. Three centuries have passed since the artist of fig. 44 painted his St. Luke. The figures in this tidy room have a sense of gravity and weight. The artist has paid particular attention to rendering the soft fur of the animal at the saint's feet. During the fifteenth century, Italian artists led the way in the creation of the new, more naturalistic painting style associated with the Renaissance.

STYLES OF MANUSCRIPT PAINTING

Manuscript painting covers a period of more than one thousand years. Inevitably, we encounter very different styles from one century to the next and from one country to the next. It is not possible to discuss all the important styles here, but some generalizations may be helpful and may make looking at these decorations more interesting.

Most of the art from the early Middle Ages—including manuscript painting—tends to depict its subjects as flat and two-dimensional, like paper dolls. Often they seem weightless or floating; they lack depth (fig. 44).

Later medieval painting is much more lifelike and naturalistic. Human figures look, move, and behave more like real people. Forms are rounded and drawn with greater anatomical accuracy. A sense of space is created by the use of perspective and by showing light falling across objects and casting shadows (fig. 45).

46. Some fifteenth-century illuminators took the fashion for a more realistic style of painting to extremes. At first glance, we are meant to think that there are real flowers, fruit—even a fly!—resting on the page of this book.

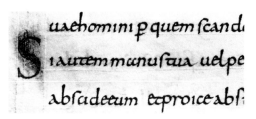

47. Uncial script, from a sixth-century manuscript.

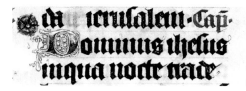

48. Carolingian minuscule script, from a ninth-century manuscript.

49. Gothic script, from an early fifteenth-century manuscript.

50. Masthead of *The New York Times*, which uses elaborate Gothic lettering.

There is a common tendency to consider paintings of these later periods better because they present a more familiar and inviting world to us. But it is important to remember that it was not necessarily the aim of early medieval artists to present a familiar and inviting world. They were following a different set of rules in which paintings of biblical events were meant to make viewers feel as if they were seeing a vision of another, more spiritual, and very mysterious world.

Over the centuries, the rules began to change. Increasingly, artists were expected to paint biblical events as if they were happening before our very eyes— almost in the same room (fig. 46). Instead of being awed and mystified by the events of Christian history, people were encouraged to perceive them in a more human and emotional way.

STYLES OF LETTERING

Just as there were changing styles in manuscript painting, so, too, there were changing styles in the kinds of writing or scripts. A person who studies scripts from long ago is called a PALEOGRAPHER (from the Greek *palaio*, ancient, and *graphia*, writing). A good paleographer can tell you the approximate date and country of a manuscript just by studying the lettering!

In manuscripts from about the fourth to the eighth century, one of the most common styles of lettering used is called UNCIAL. It is derived from the Roman style of writing, made up entirely of large capital letters formed by graceful curving strokes (fig. 47). The term *uncial* comes from the Latin *uncialis*, literally meaning inch-high.

The emperor Charlemagne was a great believer in educational reform, the spread of learning, and the production of manuscripts. During the ninth century, he authorized the use of a new, smaller, and much simpler type of handwriting for manuscripts. It was called CAROLINGIAN MINUSCULE. (*Carolingian* is the adjective to describe something relating to the reign of Charlemagne and his successors.) Carolingian minuscule was quicker to write and easier to read and was a huge success. It resembles quite closely our cursive writing of today (fig. 48).

By the twelfth century, Carolingian minuscule had been replaced by a very ornate, spiky style of handwriting called GOTHIC (fig. 49). Apparently, the term *Gothic* was given to this script later, by scholars during the Renaissance because they disliked it so much. It is, in fact, difficult to read. They called it Gothic as a mark of contempt, after the barbarian Goths. (The Goths actually had no lettering of their own.) Gothic script is still occasionally used today to make a document or title appear official or important (fig. 50).

During the fifteenth century, humanist scholars and scribes in Italy developed

a script called *ITALIC* that was very beautiful, simple, and easy to read (fig. 51). *This type of upward slanting script is still used today and is still called italic.*

The letters of the Roman alphabet were invented to write Latin, but in time, of course, English, French, and Spanish people adopted the Roman alphabet to write their spoken languages. In a similar way, the Arabic alphabet, which had been developed to write the language of the people of northern Arabia, came to be used by the many different peoples of the Islamic world to write their various languages and dialects.

As in the West, different styles of Arabic writing were used at different times and for different types of books. During the seventh century, a particularly beautiful type of Arabic script was developed for copying out the Islamic holy book, the Koran. The perfection of this lettering was a way of paying homage to God. Whether for religious or nonreligious books, the creation of an elegant, abstract design on the page is a common feature of all Arabic scripts (fig. 52).

52. Arabic script, like Hebrew writing, is read from right to left. It is composed of seventeen basic shapes, which become the twenty-eight letters of the Arabic alphabet by the addition of dots above, beneath, or within these shapes. The text explains that goats can leap from very high places and break their fall by landing on their horns!

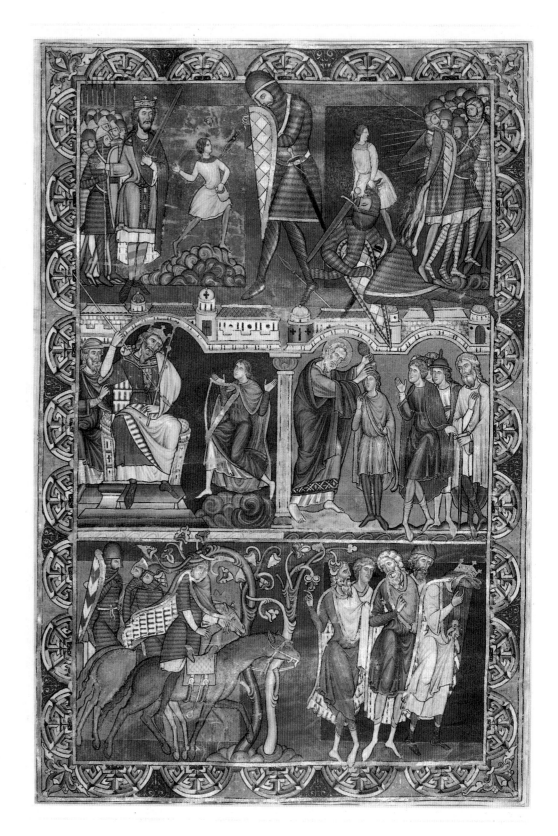

An Illuminated Bible

54. Page from a twelfth-century English Bible. At least five artists labored for more than twenty years on this Bible. Shown here are scenes from the life of David: Young David slays the giant Goliath with his sling; King Saul hurls a spear at David in a jealous rage; David is anointed King of Israel in Saul's place; David's son Absalom is caught in a tree and run through with a spear; David weeps for his dead son.

Best-Selling Books

The kinds of books people read tell us much about their lives and what they value most. Think about the subjects commonly found on today's "best-seller" lists—health and fitness, how to make and manage your money, women's issues, murder mysteries, and love stories. The Middle Ages had its best-sellers, too, and they also tell us a great deal about medieval society.

BOOKS FOR MONKS

As we know, up until the end of the twelfth century nearly all manuscripts were produced by and for the Church (fig. 53). Not surprisingly, most of these were religious texts of one sort or another. Of course, there were manuscript Bibles, but monks didn't always need copies of the entire Bible, which tended to be very large and cumbersome (fig. 54). Some parts of the scriptures were read and studied more often than others, so the sensible thing to do was simply to make manuscripts of various parts of the Bible for use where and when they were needed.

53. A monk singing at the top of his lungs, from a choir book. The scene is framed in a large initial *K*.

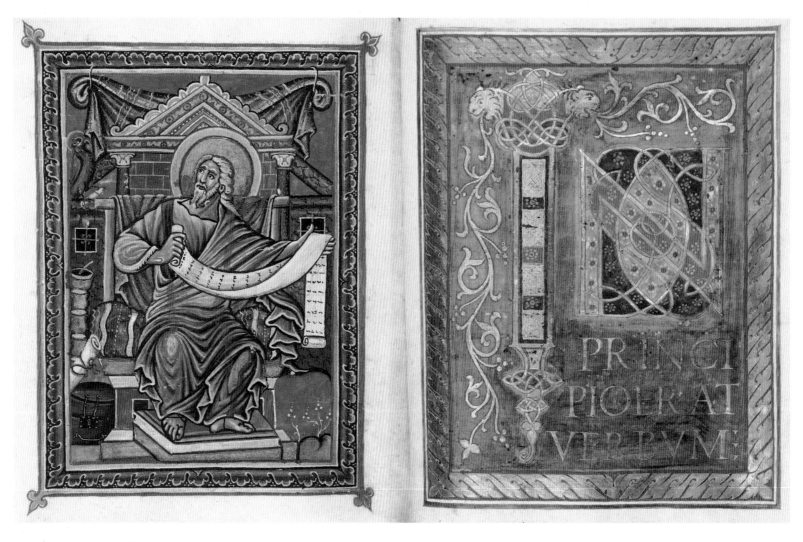

A Gospel Book from France

55. Illuminated gospel books had a fairly standard format: Each of the four sections began with a portrait of the author. On the facing page, the first letters or words (also called the incipit) of that gospel would be written in a very large and elaborate fashion. Shown here is the beginning of the Book of John from a ninth-century French gospel book. On the right-hand side, a large *I* and *N* mark the opening words of John's gospel in Latin: *In principio erat verbum* (In the beginning was the Word).

GOSPEL BOOKS   The most common type of book produced up to about the tenth century was the *GOSPEL BOOK*. This was a manuscript of the first four books of the New Testament—Matthew, Mark, Luke, and John (figs. 55–56). The gospels were regarded as the true accounts of the life and teachings of Christ. They were therefore the most important parts of the Bible for the Christian faithful of Europe. Gospel books were always carried by the early Christian missionaries, such as St. Augustine and St. Patrick, who went in search of converts among the tribes of England and Ireland. Larger and more elaborate gospel books were created for ceremonial use and were regarded as treasures of the Church (figs. 57–58).

A gospel book was more than words on a page. It was regarded as a sacred object and some were even believed to have magic, protective powers. We hear, for example, of gospel books being carried into battle to ensure victory or being used to prevent or cure disease.

Ethiopian Gospel Book

56. This Ethiopian gospel book shows St. Luke gazing upward for divine inspiration. The brilliant colors and love of patterning are typical of both Christian and non-Christian African art.

Armenian Gospel Book

57. The Armenian people of Western Asia were the earliest nation converted to Christianity. Their gospel books, often decorated in gold and a blaze of vivid colors, were cherished possessions of the Church and the community.

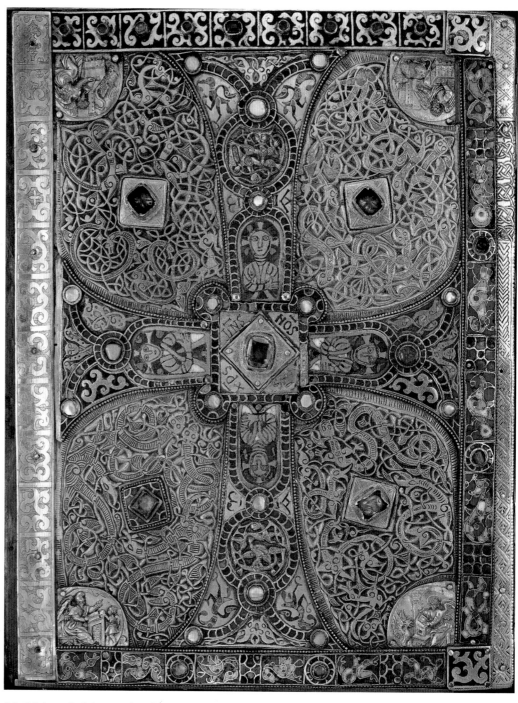

Binding for a Gospel Book

58. Rich and elaborate bindings were another way of showing the importance of a gospel book. This one, made of silver gilt, jewels, and enamels, dates from the late eighth century. The entwined serpent designs of the metalwork resemble Viking art.

Next to the gospels, the second most widely read and studied part of the Bible was the Psalms. This series of poems was believed to have been written and sung by the great Hebrew king David himself. In medieval monasteries, all 150 Psalms were meant to be recited every week, and so the *PSALTER,* a manuscript of the Book of Psalms, became a standard part of monastic life (figs. 59–60).

In addition to being used for daily prayer, Psalters may also have been used to teach young monks and nuns to read. The language is fairly simple, making the Psalter a good primer. Psalters were also produced for the laity, that is, men and women outside the Church. Many of these were decorated with delightful and amusing illustrations, which must have made daily prayers much less tedious.

A French Psalter

59. Some of the most delightful illustrations are found in Psalters. In this French Psalter, scenes from the life of David are enclosed in a large *B*, which begins the First Psalm: *Beatus vir* (Happy is the man). At the top, David is shown as an old man playing a kind of organ; below, the young David aims his sling at Goliath, who stands fearfully in the border. The borders also include a dog dressed as a pilgrim and a monkey blowing a trumpet.

in confilio impiorum: & in uia pcc
catorum non ftctit: & in cathedra pe
ftilentie non fedit.
Sed in lege domini uoluntas eius:
& in lege eius meditabit dic ac nocte.
Et erit tanquam lignum qd plan
tatum eft fecus decurfus aquaru!

The Opening of an English Psalter

60. The entire first page of this English
Psalter is taken up with the initial letter *B*
of the First Psalm. The *B* contains the
family tree of David and strange leaf men.
The rest of the word *Beatus* is spelled out
on the next page. Wise King Solomon sits
on the crossbar of the large *E*. An angel
below him swoops down with a banner
containing the rest of the letters.

A Thirteenth-Century English Apocalypse Manuscript

62. Another date prophesied for the end of the world was 1260. This English Apocalypse manuscript was produced sometime between 1255 and 1260, which was cutting it pretty close. St. Michael is shown here, battling a seven-headed beast.

A Spanish Apocalypse Manuscript

61. Giant locusts, with teeth like lions' and the stinging tails of scorpions, were but one of the horrors described in the visions of the Apocalypse or Book of Revelation. This manuscript was written in Spain about a half century before the year 1000, the year when much of Europe was convinced the prophecies of the Apocalypse would actually come to pass.

APOCALYPSES   Medieval men and women were obsessed with the horrific vision of the end of the world as prophesied in the Book of Revelation. This is the last book of the Bible, also referred to as the *APOCALYPSE*. During this final battle between good and evil, the heavens rain fire, the seas turn to blood, and giant monsters stalk the earth (fig. 61).

At certain intervals throughout the Middle Ages, some people became convinced that the fateful day was at hand—for example, the year 1000, then 1260, 1500, and so on. Inevitably, the approach of these dates would result in an increased demand for manuscripts of the Apocalypse (fig. 62).

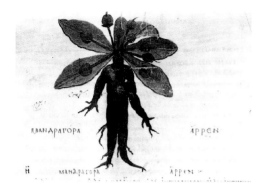

The Herbal

63. The mandrake plant is described and illustrated on this page from a tenth-century Greek herbal. Mandrake, which was used to ease pain and cause sleep, has a forked shape that can resemble the figure of a man. According to a popular medieval legend, the mandrake plant screamed when it was uprooted.

HERBALS Of course, not all the books used by monks were religious. Monasteries were also places of healing and caring for the sick. There was a practical need for books such as *HERBALS*, which explained the medicinal properties of various plants (fig. 63).

BESTIARIES Another popular book was the *BESTIARY* or book of beasts. Bestiaries recorded the habits and appearances of almost every conceivable kind of animal—from the familiar dogs, cats, and mice to the more exotic elephants, lions, and crocodiles, and even imaginary beasts (though considered very real by medieval people), such as unicorns and griffins (figs. 64–65). A strange bird called the caladrius, for example, supposedly could foretell the fate of a sick man either by looking at him or by turning its head away.

A Persian Bestiary

65. Bestiaries were common outside of Europe as well. This Persian bestiary was produced during the thirteenth century. The two elephants pictured here belong to royalty, as seen by their caps and the bells on their feet. The text explains that elephant broth is good for colds and asthma.

The Bestiary

64. The medieval bestiary was a delightful combination of fact and fable. On this page from an English bestiary we learn, for example, that a giant fish called a serra has wings and is as big as a man. It likes to fly through the air and race ships.

An Early Aesop

66. Aesop is believed to have been a Greek slave born in Thrace during the sixth century B.C. Here Aesop dreams that he has the gift of eloquent speech. This Aesop manuscript was written in Greek and illustrated during the tenth century in Italy.

There is a popular—but mistaken—notion that medieval monks completely turned their backs on the great literary and philosophical works of ancient Greece and Rome. It is true that some Church Fathers regarded the works of so-called pagan (non-Christian) authors with skepticism and even as potentially dangerous to one's soul. Nevertheless, the copying and studying of classical texts did go on in monastic scriptoria. Indeed, nearly the whole of our knowledge of ancient Greek and Roman writing comes from medieval copies. Had it not been for these diligent monks, the works of Homer, Aristotle, Plato, and Cicero, and the beloved fables of Aesop might have been lost forever (fig. 66).

Interestingly, copies of classical texts made during the early Middle Ages were usually not illustrated very much. Presumably, it was considered unnecessary or even impious to spend much time on such works. Historians have said that in monastic scriptoria when a scribe needed a Psalter to work on, he placed his hands on his head in the shape of a crown to refer to King David, but for a pagan work he would scratch himself in the manner of a dog!

BOOKS FOR THE COURT

An important change in medieval life in general and the production of manuscripts in particular began during the thirteenth century. The first universities were established around 1200, and literacy became much more widespread among the noble classes, eventually extending into the rising merchant classes as well. The demand for more and different books steadily increased. Book production moved out of the monasteries and into the world of the medieval court (fig. 67) and eventually into commercial scriptoria in cities and towns. Not surprisingly, there is a dramatic increase in the number of SECULAR (nonreligious) illuminated manuscripts. These

67. The medieval chronicler Jean Froissart presents a copy of his book to Edward III of England.

books reflect the interests and pleasures of the daily life of the nobility. Often they are written in the *vernacular*—the spoken language of the country—instead of Latin.

Stories of King Arthur

68. The first kiss of Lancelot and Guinevere. This fourteenth-century manuscript is one of the most beautifully illustrated versions of the legend of Lancelot of the Lake, Arthur's favorite knight, who fell in love with Queen Guinevere. It is written in French.

Lancelot and the Sword Bridge

69. On another page from the same manuscript as fig. 68, Lancelot must cross a sword bridge to rescue Guinevere, who is held captive in a castle. The sharp blade cuts him at every step, leaving his hands and feet bleeding.

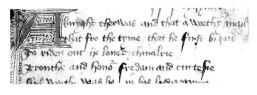

Chaucer's *Canterbury Tales*

70. Chaucer composed his famous *Canterbury Tales* six hundred years ago, and it is still one of the most widely read works in the English language. On this page from a fifteenth-century copy of the work, Chaucer introduces the Knight. The spelling seems strange to us, but when read aloud it sounds much like the English of today:

> A Knyght ther was, and that a worthy man
> That fro the tyme that he first bigan
> To riden out, he loved chivalrie,
> Trouthe and honour, fredom and curteisie.

The Sad Tale of *Troilus and Creside*

71. "The double sorrow of Troilus to tellen" begins another of Chaucer's works, *Troilus and Cresiede*. This copy was made for Henry V of England.

As early as the ninth century, the feats of King Arthur and his Knights of the Round Table had been sung and recited in the great halls of medieval castles. But it was not until the twelfth century that these beloved stories were written down and illustrated for the pleasure of the court (figs. 68–69). Today the story of Arthur is still being read all over the world and has even been made into movies and Broadway musicals.

There were also those who drew from ancient tales as well as their own experience to produce original works of literature. The idea of a writer as one who makes a living by creating rather than copying became increasingly common. In France these were called *hommes de lettres*—men of letters—but there were women, too. Christine de Pisan, who lived during the fourteenth century, is regarded as one of France's first female professional writers.

Many of the works of these medieval authors are lost to us or little read today. But others, by writers such as Dante, Boccaccio, and Petrarch in Italy, and Chaucer in England, are still among the most celebrated in world literature. Manuscripts of their works are sometimes rather plain-looking and lack elaborate decoration. It was the words that mattered most for their owners (figs. 70–71).

The subjects of these medieval literary works varied—chivalry, heroic deeds, adventure, and, above all, love. A phenomenally successful "best-seller" in France was the *Roman de la rose*—The Romance of the Rose—which tells the story of a lover's trials and adventures to win the object of his desire, a beautiful red rose (fig. 72).

A French Love Poem

72. This page begins the popular French love poem, the *Roman de la rose*—The Romance of the Rose. In it, the Lover goes to sleep; he dreams that he awakens on a beautiful May morning and dresses to go out; he follows a stream through the forest and comes to a walled garden; inside he finds the beautiful Rose. It is love at first sight.

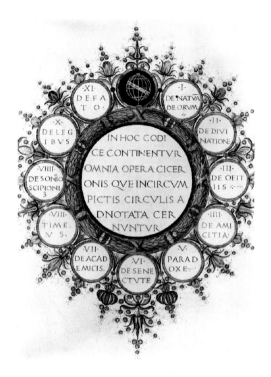

Ancient Roman Authors

73. The table of contents from a fifteenth-century copy of the works of Cicero. It was made in Florence for the rich banker and humanist Tommaso Sassetti.

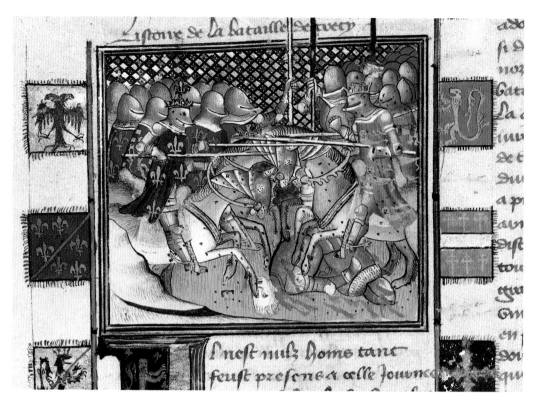

The Battle of Crécy

74. A page from Froissart's chronicle of the Hundred Years' War, describing the Battle of Crécy in 1346. Although the English soldiers (shown on the right) were greatly outnumbered by the French, they won a decisive victory because of the skill of their archers. The English were armed with longbows and could shoot much farther and faster (six times a minute) than the French with their crossbows. Both sides incurred heavy losses. Froissart tells us that over a thousand noblemen died at Crécy. The coats of arms of those who fought that day decorate the borders of the page.

In Italy, once the center of the empire of ancient Rome, there was a great renewal of interest in classical learning and literature. Works by the great Greek and Roman writers, which had been lying hidden away in monastic libraries, were now copied in elegant volumes for the libraries of Renaissance princes and scholars (fig. 73).

There was also a growing curiosity about contemporary events, people, and places, and this, too, is reflected in books of the late Middle Ages. The Hundred Years' War (from about 1337 to 1453) affected the lives of nearly every noble house of France and England. A fourteenth-century Frenchman named Jean Froissart wrote an incredibly detailed account of this period and has gone down in history as one of the first war journalists. His chronicle was exceedingly popular in his own time and is still studied carefully by historians today (fig. 74).

75. The strange people of Traponce, who live in the shells of giant snails. From a fifteenth-century French manuscript, *Le Livre des merveilles du monde*—The Book of the Marvels of the World.

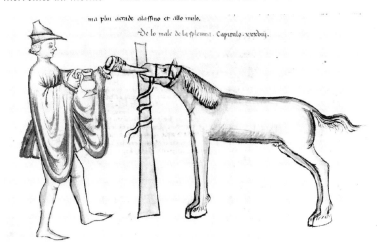

76. Page from a fifteenth-century Italian manuscript on the care of sick horses.

The Uses of Armor

77. A fifteenth-century English manuscript describes the types of armor needed for fighting on foot. The young squire is tying on a coat of mail, which goes under the breastplate. The text under the illustration is in Middle English and reads: "How a man schall be armyd at his ese when he schal fighte on foote."

Marco Polo's account of his travels (from 1271 to 1295) in China and other lands along the Silk Route was one of the earliest detailed descriptions of the Far East by a European. His book was translated into many languages and helped set a fashion for other books describing the "wonders of the world." A lot of these were works more of fantasy than fact, but they must have helped many a courtier pass long winter nights in wide-eyed amazement (fig. 75).

BOOKS TO EXPLAIN   In addition to books for entertainment and intellectual enlightenment, there were practical "how-to" books (fig. 76). Books on warfare described and illustrated the different types of armor and weapons for jousting and battle (fig. 77).

The Stag Hunt

78. This miniature from Gaston Phébus's *Livre de la chasse* shows the moment when a stag has been spotted. Phébus himself raises the ivory hunting horn and sounds the signal for the hounds to give chase. The servants stand by with their lances, ready to go in for the kill.

A Medieval Doghouse

79. Dogs being kenneled and fed, from Gaston Phébus's *Livre de la chasse*.

A favorite pastime of the medieval court was hunting, and there were books on how to track and hunt game. One of the most famous of these was the *Livre de la chasse*—The Book of the Hunt. It was written by Gaston Phébus, a French knight famed for his courage as a soldier as well as his skill as a hunter (fig. 78). He was also a great lover of dogs (at one point he is said to have owned over sixteen hundred), and several chapters of his book deal with the proper way to breed, care for, and train dogs (fig. 79).

Adults are always trying to impress upon children the need for courteous and proper behavior. It was no different in the Middle Ages, and there were books for noble children explaining courtly etiquette and principles of religious piety and moral behavior. These deal with the need to eat the proper foods, avoid bad company, and show respect and obedience for one's parents (fig. 80). Sounds familiar, doesn't it?

BOOKS OF HOURS   Although secular manuscripts, like the *Canterbury Tales*, the *Livre de la chasse*, and the Arthur stories, were enormously popular during the later Middle Ages, the single most widely produced type of book during this period was a series of prayers known as the BOOK OF HOURS. As its name implies, this consisted of various prayers and readings to be recited at specific times, or hours, of the day (fig. 81).

Proper Behavior

80. A fourteenth-century French manuscript instructs young princes on their duties. Two obedient children kneel before their royal parents.

The Book of Hours

81. "The Holy Family at Work," from a Dutch Book of Hours in Latin. The scene illustrates the prayer to be recited at noon, the hour called *sext*. Everyone is busy: Mary weaves; Joseph planes wood; and the infant Jesus learns to walk.

The Torments of Hell

82. Books of Hours always contained prayers for the dead, sometimes accompanied by a picture of the Mouth of Hell that was meant to be as horrifying as possible, an admonition to readers to mend their ways. Here the entrance to hell is imagined as three giant cat-like heads.

Death could come swiftly and with no warning during the Middle Ages. Daily prayer from a Book of Hours was a kind of "life insurance" against going to hell. Often these books were quite small (some measure only a few inches square) so that they could be slipped in a pocket and carried about (fig. 82).

The Book of Hours usually began with the calendar, in which the feast days for each month were written. Especially holy dates were written in gold or red, hence our term *red-letter day*, meaning a day of great importance. Each of the months was also illustrated with scenes from everyday life during the changing seasons (figs. 83–84).

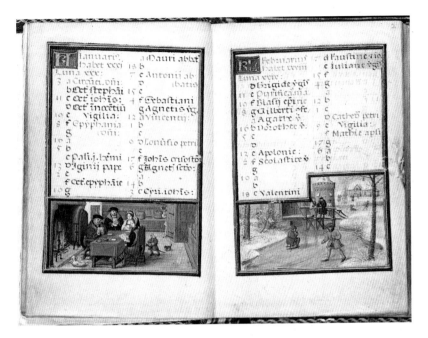

Pastimes of the Winter Months

83. The calendar pages for January and February from a Book of Hours. The bottom of each page is illustrated with favorite pastimes for these months—playing cards by the fire and skating. You may need a magnifying glass to make out all the details of these scenes. This tiny Book of Hours is reproduced here in its actual size, and the artist undoubtedly used magnification to paint the illustrations.

All who could afford such an expense had one or more Books of Hours made for them, and it is rightly referred to as *the* late medieval best-seller. Just as Psalters had been used to teach young monks to read, some Books of Hours were undoubtedly used to teach children to read. Often elaborate and beautifully illuminated, they became a symbol of wealth and status. Commonly we find the owners of Books of Hours proudly including self-portraits and other references to themselves and their social status in the manuscript (fig. 85).

The Merry Month of May

84. Illustration for May, from a Book of Hours. Spring was a time to be outside and make merry. Young couples pass the day gliding down a canal in a boat, their cask of wine hanging over the side to cool in the water. In the background, a group of riders has just emerged from the forest, and they are making their way to a thatched-roof cottage.

85. This is the opening page from a Book of Hours made for the Dutch noble-woman Catherine of Cleves. Catherine herself is shown kneeling on the left, dressed in red velvet robes lined with ermine. In her hands she holds a Book of Hours. The borders are decorated with the coats of arms of Catherine's family and those of her husband, Arnold of Guelders. We should not be fooled by Catherine's gentle and pious appearance here. An ambitious and ruthless woman, she later had her husband imprisoned in an effort to take over his kingdom.

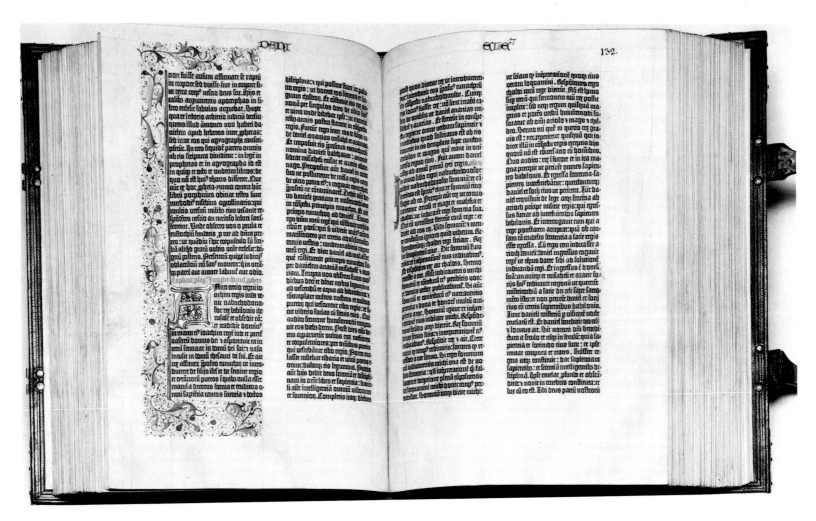

The Dawn of the Printed Book

86. A page from a copy of the Gutenberg Bible, the first book printed with movable type, from about 1455. Despite the obvious advantages of printing, many people still preferred to have their books made the old-fashioned way, by hand. It is interesting to see how Gutenberg tried to imitate the way illuminated manuscripts looked in his printed Bibles. Ruling lines, unnecessary on a printed page, were drawn in. Borders and initial letters were still decorated by hand.

The Invention of Printing

If the Middle Ages began with a new way of making books—the codex—then it also ended with a new way of making books—with the invention of printing in about 1455. Credit for this invention goes to Johann Gutenberg, a German goldsmith who perfected a way to make individual metal letters—movable type—that could be arranged to form a page of text, inked, and then pressed onto a surface. Any mistakes could be corrected by moving the type around. And when as many copies as were needed had been made, the letters could be taken apart and reassembled for the next page. The first complete book from Gutenberg's press was the Bible, in Latin (fig. 86).

The advantages of printing were obvious. One man could print more pages in a day than a scribe could write in a year and without the same risk of mistakes. Yet many people still preferred to have illuminated manuscripts. The practice of copying and illustrating books by hand continued for more than a century after the first Gutenberg Bibles appeared. This may strike us today as strange, but it is important to understand that, during the Middle Ages, books were valued not just for their information and the words they contained. Books were meant to be beautiful and to look a certain way. Think back to the centuries it took for the codex to catch on, even though it was much more practical than the scroll.

Gutenberg and the other early printers clearly understood this, and took pains to make their books look as much like manuscript volumes as possible. What these early printers could not do, however, was print beautiful full-color illustrations. Perhaps this is why the illuminated manuscripts produced after the invention of printing were often even more elaborately painted and decorated (fig. 87). Such books were truly luxury items, more like portable art galleries.

Eventually, however, the printed book won out over the illuminated manuscript. Then and only then could books really become, as they are today, part of our daily lives.

87. Lavishly illustrated manuscripts continued to be made for more than a century following the invention of printing. This Italian Book of Hours was made in 1546. The artist, Giulio Clovio, was a contemporary of the great Renaissance painter Michelangelo.

About the Pierpont Morgan Library

Both a museum and a center for scholarly research, the Pierpont Morgan Library originated with the medieval and Renaissance manuscripts, rare books and fine bindings, autograph manuscripts, and master drawings collected by J. Pierpont Morgan (1837–1913). In 1890, Morgan began to assemble a collection that rivaled the great libraries of Europe. In 1924, J. P. Morgan, Jr., transformed the library into a public institution as a memorial to his father's "love of rare books and manuscripts and his belief in the educational value of the collections."

The Library's collection of illuminated manuscripts is now considered the finest outside Europe. In addition to making these materials available for scholarly research, the Library regularly includes them in public exhibitions. The purpose of this book is, therefore, twofold: to provide a basic introduction to the art and history of manuscript illumination and to share the Library's exceptional holdings in this field.

Ranging from the fifth century through the late Renaissance, the Library's holdings of Latin (i.e., Christian) manuscripts from Western Europe encompass nearly all the major schools and periods of European manuscript illumination. Yet there are gaps, which are inevitably reflected in this volume. Because most were already in public collections, J. Pierpont Morgan had little opportunity to acquire important late antique, early Christian, or early Anglo-Irish (Hiberno-Saxon) manuscripts. There are also few examples from the very long and rich tradition of Hebrew manuscript illumination.

The Library does, however, own a number of significant non-Western (i.e., Indian, Persian, and Arabic) manuscripts. Examples from some have been included to suggest parallel developments and achievements by non-European cultures.

Glossary

APOCALYPSE
The last book of the Bible, also called the Book of Revelation. According to Christian belief, it was written by St. John the Evangelist and describes visions of the final, cataclysmic battle between good and evil that he experienced on the island of Patmos.

BESTIARY
A book containing myth and folklore about real and imaginary animals.

BOOK OF HOURS
A prayer book intended for use by the laity that had at its core a series of prayers to the Virgin Mary. These consist of eight sections to be recited at eight specified times, or "hours," during the day—from Matins in the morning to Compline in the evening.

CAROLINGIAN MINUSCULE
A style of clear, round script that was developed during the late eighth century under the patronage of the emperor Charlemagne.

CODEX
The book form as we know it today, consisting of individual pages sewn or glued along one edge, which can be turned one after another. The codex replaced the papyrus scroll at least in part because it was more practical for recitation, cross-referencing, and storage.

GOSPEL BOOK
A volume of the first four books of the New Testament, the gospel writings of Matthew, Mark, Luke, and John. Up to about the tenth century, this was the single most common type of manuscript produced in the Christian world.

GOTHIC
A term generally used to describe the art and culture of medieval Europe from about the middle of the twelfth century to the early sixteenth century. The word was coined by Renaissance scholars, who regarded this period as much less civilized than their own and likened it to the barbarian culture of the Goths.

HERBAL
A book giving the names, descriptions, and uses of various plants.

HISTORIATED INITIAL
An initial letter in which a small scene has been painted.

ILLUMINATED MANUSCRIPT
A book in codex form that is written and illustrated by hand.

ILLUMINATION
The hand-painted decoration in a manuscript. The frequent use of precious metals that glitter and reflect light is the source of the term, which derives from the Latin *illuminare*, to light up. *Illumination* now denotes any type of painted decoration, whether or not precious metals are used.

ITALIC
A style of lettering derived from the sloped cursive script used by humanists of the Italian Renaissance. Italic type is used today in printing for emphasis or to indicate a book title.

KORAN
The sacred book of Islam. According to the Islamic faith, it contains the words of God as made known to the prophet Mohammed by the angel Gabriel, beginning around A.D. 610 and continuing for about twenty years.

LATIN
The spoken and written language of ancient Rome, which became the official language of the Western Christian Church during the Middle Ages.

MANUSCRIPT
Any text written by hand. The term comes from the Latin words *manus* (hand) and *scribere* (to write).

MONASTERY
A house for persons living under religious vows. The term comes from the Greek *monazein*, to live alone.

PALEOGRAPHY
The study of ancient writing. By examining the manner in which the characters are made, a paleographer can establish the date of a manuscript and the place in which it was produced.

PARCHMENT
See *Vellum.*

PSALTER
A manuscript of the Book of Psalms, used for private prayer or for readings in church services.

SCRIBE
The person who writes out the text of manuscripts, from the Latin *scribere*, to write.

SCRIPTORIUM
The special room set aside for the production of manuscripts.

SECULAR
Not specifically religious in content or purpose.

TORAH
The first five books of the Hebrew Bible, also referred to as the Pentateuch.

UNCIAL
The style of lettering commonly used in manuscripts from about the fourth to the eighth century A.D.

VELLUM
Specially prepared animal skin used to make the pages of manuscripts. The term *vellum* is used interchangeably with *parchment.*

VERNACULAR
The native language or dialect of a particular country or region (for example, French, in France).

Illustrations

32. St. Matthew. Book of Hours, in Latin, France, Aix-en-Provence, ca. 1445, by Barthélemy van Eyck (M.358, f.17)

33. Rabbit doctor and two patients. Book of Hours, in Latin, France, Aix-en-Provence, ca. 1445, by Barthélemy van Eyck (M.358, f.20v, det.)

34. St. Philip. Book of Hours ("Hours of Catherine of Cleves"), in Latin, The Netherlands, Utrecht, ca. 1440, by the Master of Catherine of Cleves, for Catherine of Cleves, duchess of Guelders (M.917, p.226, det.)

35. Nativity, in an initial P. Single leaf from a Gradual, in Latin, Italy, Florence, Monastery of Santa Maria degli Angeli, ca. 1365–1400, by Silvestro dei Gherarducci and workshop (M.653, f.1)

36. David anointed, in an initial D. Psalter ("Windmill Psalter"), in Latin, England, probably London, ca. 1290 (M.102, f.24v)

37. Man beating gold. Single leaf, probably from a register of creditors of a Bolognese lending society, in Latin, Italy, Bologna, ca. 1390–1400, by Nicolò da Bologna (M.1056, f.2, det.)

38. Text pages. Book of Hours, in Latin, France, Aix-en-Provence, ca. 1445 (M.358, ff.169v–170)

39. St. Martin dividing his cloak, St. Martin raising three dead; decorated initial D. Sacramentary ("Berthold Sacramentary"), in Latin, Germany, Weingarten Abbey, ca. 1200–32, by the Master of the Berthold Sacramentary (M.710, ff.125v–126)

40. Marriage of the Virgin, surrounded by medallions with scenes from the life of the Virgin. Book of Hours, in Latin, Paris, ca. 1420, by the Master of Morgan 453 (M.453, f.30v)

41. European-style sewing and attachment to boards, on cords and thongs. On a Sacramentary, in Latin for the Cathedral of Urgel, Spain, Catalonia, Urgel, ca. 1150 (M.922)

42. Jewish bookbinding from Provence, after 1422. On a Hebrew Bible, copied out by Simeon ben Samuel, 1422 (G.48, FC)

43. Gilt silver and jeweled book cover. Original cover of the "Berthold Sacramentary," in Latin, Germany, Weingarten Abbey, ca. 1200–32. (M.710, FC)

44. St. Luke. Gospels, in Latin, England, ca. 1130 (M.777, f.37v)

45. St. Luke painting the Virgin. Prayer book, in Latin, Italy, Milan, ca. 1420, by Michelino da Besozzo (M.944, f.75v, det.)

46. Detail of border, from the Coronation of the Virgin. Book of Hours, in Latin, Belgium or France, ca. 1480, by Simon Marmion (M.6, f.57v, det.)

47. Text page. Pliny the Younger, Epistolae (fragment), in Latin, Italy, early sixth century (M.462, f.3, det.)

48. Text page. Gospels, in Latin, France, Monastery of St. Martin at Tours, ninth century (M.191, f.44v, det.)

49. Text page. St. Thomas Aquinas, Office of the Holy Sacrament, in Latin, Austria, Vienna, ca. 1403–06 (M.853, f.2, det.)

50. Masthead of The New York Times. Copyright © 1994 by The New York Times Company. Reprinted by permission.

51. Text page. Marcus Valerius Martialis, Epigrammata, in Latin, Italy, probably Rome, ca. 1480 (M.946, f.182, det.)

52. Goats. Abu Bakhtishu, Manafi al-Hayawan (Uses of Animals), in Persian, Naskhi script, Persia, Maragha, ca. 1290–1300 (M.500, f.37v)

53. Monk singing, in an initial K. Psalter and Book of Hours, in Latin and French, northern France, probably the vicinity of Amiens, ca. 1290, for Yolande de Soissons (M.729, f.196, det.)

54. Scenes from the life of David. Single leaf from a Bible ("Winchester Bible"), England, Winchester, Cathedral Priory of St. Swithin, ca. 1160–80, by Master of the Morgan Leaf (M.619, v)

55. St. John: Incipit of John. Gospels, in Latin, France, Reims, during the time of Archbishop Hincmar, ca. 860 (M.728, ff.141v–142)

56. St. Luke. Gospels, in Ethiopic, Ethiopia, dated August 29, 1400, to August 28, 1401, for Princess Zir Ganela (M.828, f.108v)

57. Colophon. Gospels ("Marshal Oshin Gospels"), in Armenian, Cilicia, Sis, dated 1274 (M.740, f.6v)

58. Gilt silver, enamel, and jeweled book cover. Lower cover (southern Germany?; late eighth century; M.1, LC) of a Gospels ("Lindau Gospels"), Abbey of St. Gall, Switzerland, late ninth century.

59. Beatus page with David scenes, in an initial B and in borders. Psalter and Book of Hours, in Latin and French, northern France, probably the vicinity of Amiens, ca. 1290, for Yolande de Soissons (M.729, f.16)

60. Beatus page with Tree of Jesse, Creation scenes, and Evangelists; Judgment of Solomon, in an initial E. Psalter ("Windmill Psalter"), in Latin, England, probably London, ca. 1290 (M.102, ff.1v–2)

61. Fifth trumpet: men stung by locusts (Rev. 9:7–12). Beatus of Liébana, Commentary on the Apocalypse, and Jerome, Commentary on Daniel, in Latin, Spain, province of León, probably San Salvador de Tábara, ca. 950, by Maius for Abbot Victor of San Miguel de Escalada (M.644, f.142v)

62. St. Michael battling the seven-headed beast. Apocalypse Picture Book, in Latin, England, London, probably Westminster Abbey, ca. 1255–60 (M.524, f.8v, det.)

63. Mandrake. Dioscorides Pedanius, De materia medica, in Greek, Constantinople, ca. 950 (M.652, f.103v)

64. Serra flying over a boat. Bestiary ("Worksop Bestiary"), in Latin, England, possibly Lincoln or York, before 1187 (M.81, f.69)

65. Two elephants. Abu Bakhtishu, Manafi al-Hayawan (Uses of Animals), in Persian, Persia, Maragha, ca. 1290–1300 (M.500, f.13)

66. Aesop dreaming he can speak fluently. Aesop, Life and Fables, and other texts, in Greek, southern Italy, tenth or eleventh century (M.397, f.24)

67. Froissart presenting his book to a king, possibly Edward III. Jean Froissart, Chroniques, in French, France, Paris, ca. 1412, by the workshop of the Master of the Berry Apocalypse, for Pierre de Fontenoy (M.804, f.1)

68. First kiss of Lancelot and Guinevere, Senechal conversing with the Lady of Malohaut and Laura of Carduel. Le Roman de Lancelot du Lac, in French, northeastern France, early fourteenth century (M.805, f.67)

69. Lancelot rescuing Guinevere by crossing the sword bridge. *Le Roman de Lancelot du Lac,* in French, northeastern France, early fourteenth century (M.805, f.166)

70. Prologue. Geoffrey Chaucer, *Canterbury Tales,* in English, England, ca. 1455 (M.249, f.2v, det.)

71. Beginning of Book I. Geoffrey Chaucer, *Troilus and Cresiede,* in English, England, ca. 1399–1413, possibly for Henry V when he was prince of Wales (M.817, f.2)

72. The Lover asleep, rising, listening to the birds by the stream, and entering the garden gate. Guillaume de Lorris and Jean de Meun, *Roman de la rose,* in French, France, ca. 1350 (M.324, f.1)

73. Decorated frontispiece. Cicero, *Marcus Tullius,* in Latin, Italy, Florence, ca. 1470s, for Tommaso Sassetti (M.497, frontispiece)

74. Battle of Crécy (August 26, 1346). Jean Froissart, *Chroniques,* in French, France, Paris, ca. 1412, by the workshop of the Master of the Berry Apocalypse, for Pierre de Fontenoy (M.804, f.101v)

75. Traponce, where people live in shells. *Le Livre des merveilles du monde,* in French, France, probably Angers, ca. 1460, from the circle of the Master of Jouvenel des Ursins (M.461, f.78, det.)

76. Treatment of a horse. Bonifacio di Calabria, *Libro de la menescalcia degli cavalli,* in Italian and Latin, southern Italy, ca. 1400–25 (M.735, f.75v, det.)

77. Arming a man for fighting on foot. *Ordinances of Armoury, Jousting, Sword and Axe Combat, and Chivalry,* in English, England, ca. 1450, for Sir John Astley (M.775, f.122v)

78. Stag hunt. Gaston Phébus, *Livre de la chasse,* in French, France, Paris, ca. 1410 (M.1044, f.76)

79. Dogs being kenneled and fed. Gaston Phébus, *Livre de la chasse,* in French, France, Paris, ca. 1410 (M.1044, f.43v)

80. Respect that children owe to parents. *Avis aus Roys,* in French, France, possibly Paris, ca. 1360 (M.456, f.74)

81. The Holy Family at Work. Book of Hours ("Hours of Catherine of Cleves"), in Latin, The Netherlands, Utrecht, ca. 1440, by the Master of Catherine of Cleves, for Catherine of Cleves, duchess of Guelders (M.917, p.149)

82. Mouth of Hell; Office of the Dead. Book of Hours ("Hours of Catherine of Cleves"), in Latin, The Netherlands, Utrecht, ca. 1440, by the Master of Catherine of Cleves, for Catherine of Cleves, duchess of Guelders (M.945, ff.168v–169)

83. January and February. Book of Hours, in Latin, Belgium, Bruges, ca. 1520, by Simon Bening (M.307, ff.1v–2)

84. May: boating scene. Book of Hours ("Da Costa Hours"), in Latin, Belgium, Bruges, ca. 1515, by Simon Bening and others (M.399, f.6v)

85. Catherine of Cleves kneeling before the Virgin and Child. Book of Hours ("Hours of Catherine of Cleves"), in Latin, The Netherlands, Utrecht, ca. 1440, by the Master of Catherine of Cleves, for Catherine of Cleves, duchess of Guelders (M.945, f.1v)

86. *Biblia Latina.* (Mainz: Johann Gutenberg and Johann Fust, ca. 1455). (PML 818, ff.131v–132)

87. Coronation of the Virgin; Coronation of Esther. Book of Hours ("Farnese Hours"), in Latin, Italy, Rome, 1546, by Giulio Clovio, for Cardinal Alessandro Farnese (M.69, ff.48v–49)

Acknowledgments

Many people were crucial to this publication. William Voelkle, the Library's curator of medieval and Renaissance manuscripts, not only caught errors and omissions but also made invaluable suggestions. I am also grateful to Charles E. Pierce, Jr., and Brian Regan for their support as well as to Margaret Grant for her comments and criticism.

Thanks are owed to Lenny Hort, editor; Melissa Mead of Farrar, Straus and Giroux; and designers Klaus Gemming and Eric Marshall. Christopher de Hamel's *A History of Illuminated Manuscripts* and *Scribes and Illuminators* both proved to be highly useful sources.

Library staff members—past and present—deserving special mention include Carla Berry, Noah Chasin, Inge Dupont, Patricia Emerson, Julianne Griffin, Mimi Hollanda, Grace Lappin, David A. Loggie, Kathleen Luhrs, Anita Masi, Carolyn Nesbitt, Marilyn Palmeri, Nancy Schmugge, Frederick Schroeder, Edward Sowinski, and Lynn Thommen.

Funding was provided in part by grants from the National Endowment for the Arts, a federal agency, and the Joseph H. and Florence A. Roblee Foundation.

To Learn More

J. J. G. ALEXANDER
Medieval Illuminators and Their Methods of Work, New Haven and
    London, 1992.
J. BACKHOUSE
The Illuminated Manuscript, London, 1979.
C. DE HAMEL
A History of Illuminated Manuscripts, Boston, 1986.
C. DE HAMEL
Scribes and Illuminators, Toronto and Buffalo, 1992.

L. GOLD, ed.
*A Sign and a Witness: 2,000 Years of Hebrew Books and Illuminated
    Manuscripts,* New York and Oxford, 1988.
D. GOLDSTEIN
Hebrew Manuscript Painting, London, 1985.
O. PACHT
Book Illumination in the Middle Ages, Oxford and New York, 1986.
W. VOELKLE
Masterpieces of Medieval Painting, Chicago, 1980.

PUBLIC COLLECTIONS OF
ILLUMINATED MANUSCRIPTS IN
THE UNITED STATES

This list is not meant to be complete but gives some of the principal public institutions that own and display illuminated manuscripts. Visits should be preceded by a call to make sure that manuscripts are currently being displayed.

Beinecke Rare Book and Manuscript Library
Yale University
121 Wall Street
New Haven, Connecticut 06520

The Brooklyn Museum
200 Eastern Parkway
Brooklyn, New York 11238

The Cloisters
(a branch of the Metropolitan Museum of Art)
Fort Tryon Park
New York, New York 10040

The J. Paul Getty Museum
17985 Pacific Coast Highway
Malibu, California 90265

Huntington Library, Art Collections and Botanical Gardens
1151 Oxford Road
San Marino, California 91108

The Metropolitan Museum of Art
Fifth Avenue at 82d Street
New York, New York 10028

The Pierpont Morgan Library
29 East 36th Street
New York, New York 10016

The Walters Art Gallery
600 North Charles Street
Baltimore, Maryland 21201